LET'S LEARN
GOOD MANNERS

Thank you!

By Julie Li

This book is dedicated to all the kiddies learning to navigate the world.
May you always be kind to each other and make life more beautiful.

This book
belongs to:

_____

Reading is so much fun!

Harry Hedgehog and Brandon Bear
see each other. What do they say?

Polly Pig is leaving grandma's house after dinner.
What do they say to each other?

Crystal Cat got a lollipop from her mommy.
What does she say?

Bella Bunny is so hungry.

What does she say?

Robbie Raccoon and Benjamin Bunny are in class with their teacher Ms. Owl. What do they do?

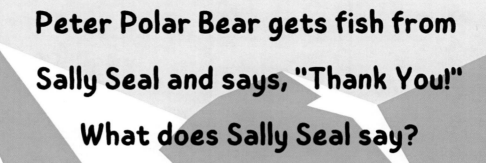

Peter Polar Bear gets fish from Sally Seal and says, "Thank You!"
What does Sally Seal say?

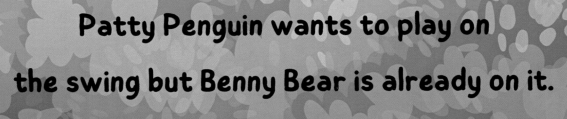

Patty Penguin wants to play on the swing but Benny Bear is already on it. What will she do?

Tessa Mouse loves balloons.
What will Kayla kitten do?

Percy Panda finished playing with his toys. What will he do?

Harriet Hippo is playing with her toys. Ollie Otter wants to play too. What will Ollie Otter say?

Sorry

Rasa Rabbit is very tired from rowing the boat.

What should Ferri Fox do?

Lilia and Serena are coughing and sneezing. What should they do?

Grandma Fox is in the subway car
but she has no seat.
What should Ariana Mouse do?

Let's review our good manners!

1. What do you say when you see your friend?

2. What do you say when you leave grandma's house?

3. What do you do when you sneeze or cough?

4. What do you do when your teacher speaks?

5. What do you say if you want to play with someone's toys?

6. What do you say if you step on your friend's toes?

7. What do you do when you are done playing with your toys?

8. What do you say when someone gives you a present?

9. What do you do if you have extra lollipops and your friend has none?

Can you tell me how

you showed good manners?

We hope you enjoy reading this!
Other books by Julie Li on www.sunsparkmedia.com

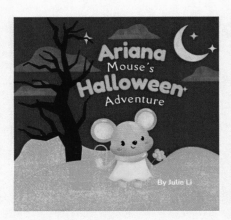

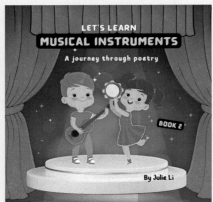

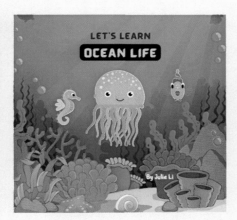

"The more that you read, the more things you will know. The more that you learn, the more places you'll go."

Dr. Seuss

Made in United States
North Haven, CT
11 July 2023

38819007R00022